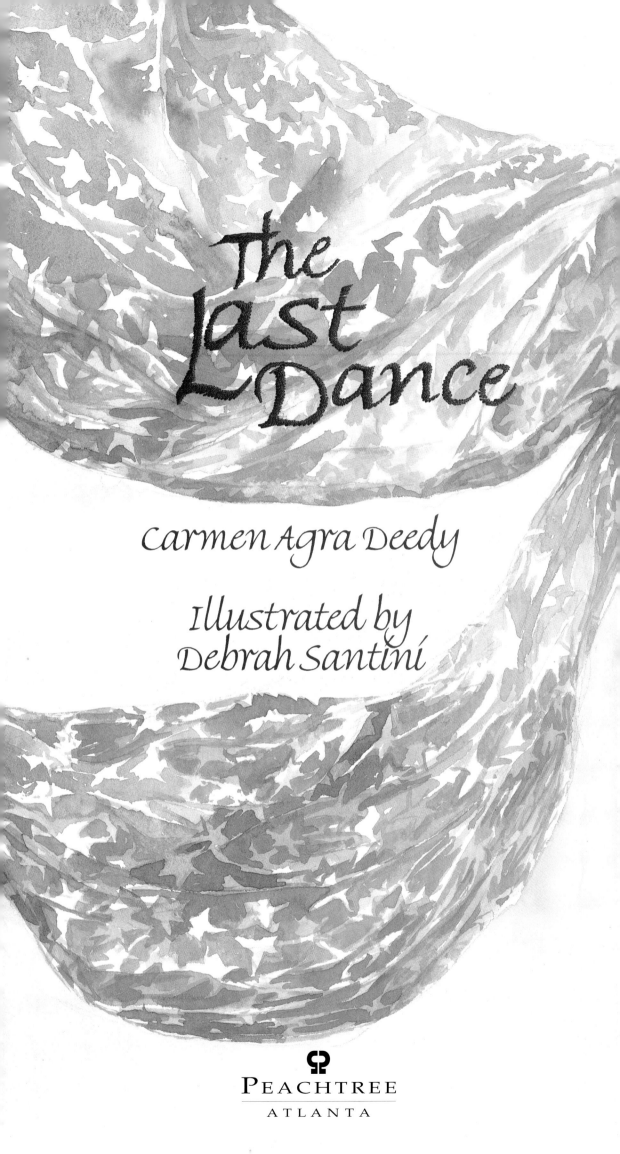

The Last Dance

Carmen Agra Deedy

Illustrated by
Debrah Santini

PEACHTREE
ATLANTA

This story is in memory of
my Tía Coralía and
my Tío J. Luís Cabrera,
and for all the Ninnys and Bessies
who may have occasionally missed the steps,
but never left The Dance.

Para mí famíglía,
Sara, Emílío, Madeline e Ann,
for their love
and encouragement.
Rom. 12:6.

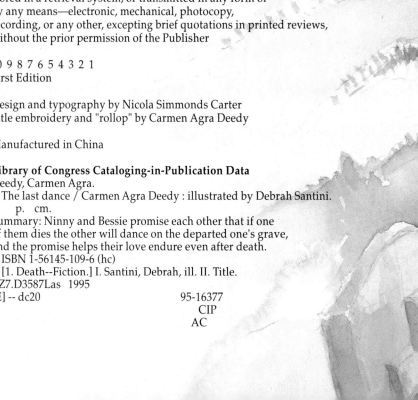

And for John and Lee Bernd in memory of
their forty-three years together.

PUBLISHED BY
Peachtree Publishers, Ltd.
494 Armour Circle, N.E.
Atlanta, Georgia 30324

Text © 1995 by Carmen Agra Deedy
Illustrations © 1995 by Debrah Santini

10 9 8 7 6 5 4 3 2 1
First Edition

Design and typography by Nicola Simmonds Carter
Title embroidery and "rollop" by Carmen Agra Deedy

Manufactured in China

Library of Congress Cataloging-in-Publication Data
Deedy, Carmen Agra.
  The last dance / Carmen Agra Deedy : illustrated by Debrah Santini.
     p. cm.
Summary: Ninny and Bessie promise each other that if one
of them dies the other will dance on the departed one's grave,
and the promise helps their love endure even after death.
  ISBN 1-56145-109-6 (hc)
  [1. Death--Fiction.] I. Santini, Debrah, ill. II. Title.
PZ7.D3587Las 1995
[E] -- dc20   95-16377
                                        CIP
                                        AC

Ninny would throw
buttons at my window:
his grandfather was a tailor.

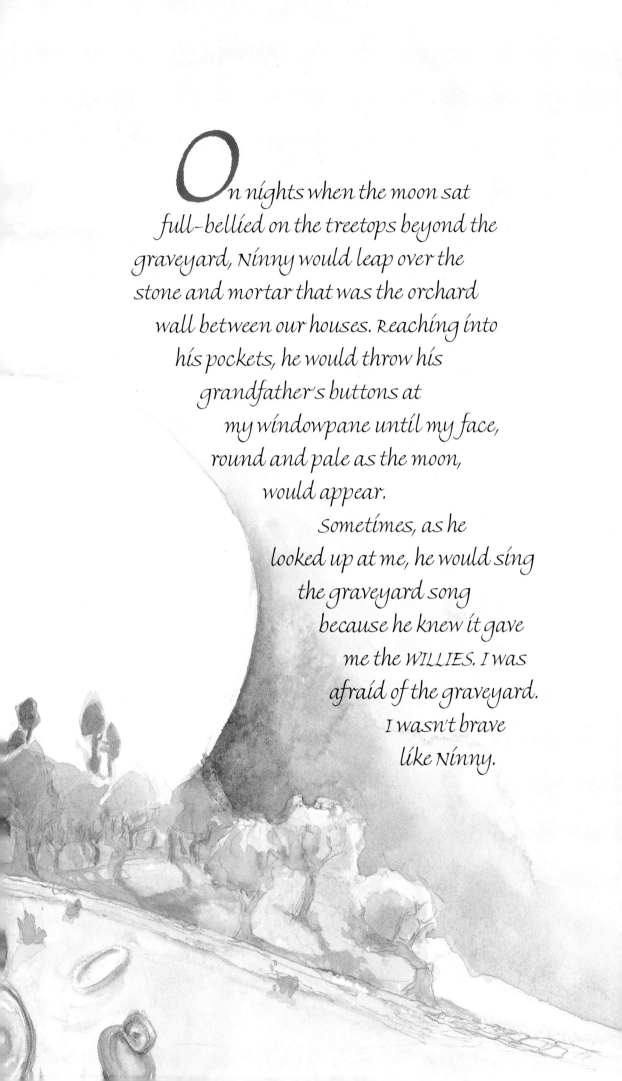

On nights when the moon sat
full-bellied on the treetops beyond the
graveyard, Ninny would leap over the
stone and mortar that was the orchard
wall between our houses. Reaching into
his pockets, he would throw his
grandfather's buttons at
my windowpane until my face,
round and pale as the moon,
would appear.
Sometimes, as he
looked up at me, he would sing
the graveyard song
because he knew it gave
me the WILLIES. I was
afraid of the graveyard.
I wasn't brave
like Ninny.

I can still hear his merry voice
ringing out like a chapel bell—

Bessie! Oh, Bessie!
Come dance with me!
      For I hate to dance alone,
where the old men sleep,
            And the women weep,
            And the wild, fey
                  children roam.

I, in my nightgown full of
stars, shivered with delight as I
shimmied down the drainpipe to
meet Ninny. He, in his pajamas of a
bilious green, waited below—
      grinning wickedly and
      clutching his
            grandfather's pipe.

To the graveyard we would go. Ninny's
grandfather, Oppa, slept there—Row seven, Grave
three. Ninny never feared the graveyard. He said
any place that Oppa sleeps is a good place.
Under a fleet of stars, Ninny would dance
and play his pipe and I would waltz with
shadows and sing.

Then we would tell stories about Oppa.
When Oppa was alive, we used to walk
the path with him to the graveyard to visit
Nana, his wife.

Once, when Ninny
made fun of my squeaky
voice, I laughed at the funny
way he danced. That night
Oppa taught us that every
human being has the right
to three things:

To dance. The great thing in life
is not so much to dance well, but whether
one is willing to dance at all.

To sing, even if you sing
off-key. The crow has as much
right to a voice as the nightingale.

To tell stories. Those we
love are never really gone as long as
their stories are told.

After Oppa was gone, Ninny and I would often
slip away to visit him at the graveyard.

On one of those milk-moon nights, Ninny put
down his pipe and began to dance a jig. For Oppa.

He was a wild and beautiful thing to watch as
his lanky body cast moon shadows across crooked
gravestones.

When he dropped exhausted at my feet, I knelt
next to him and whispered, "Ninny, when I die, I want
you to come to the graveyard and dance on my grave."

"Oh, yes," he said, breathless,
"but you must promise to do the
same for me."
Having struck a
bargain, we
crossed our
hearts, spit,
and shook
hands.

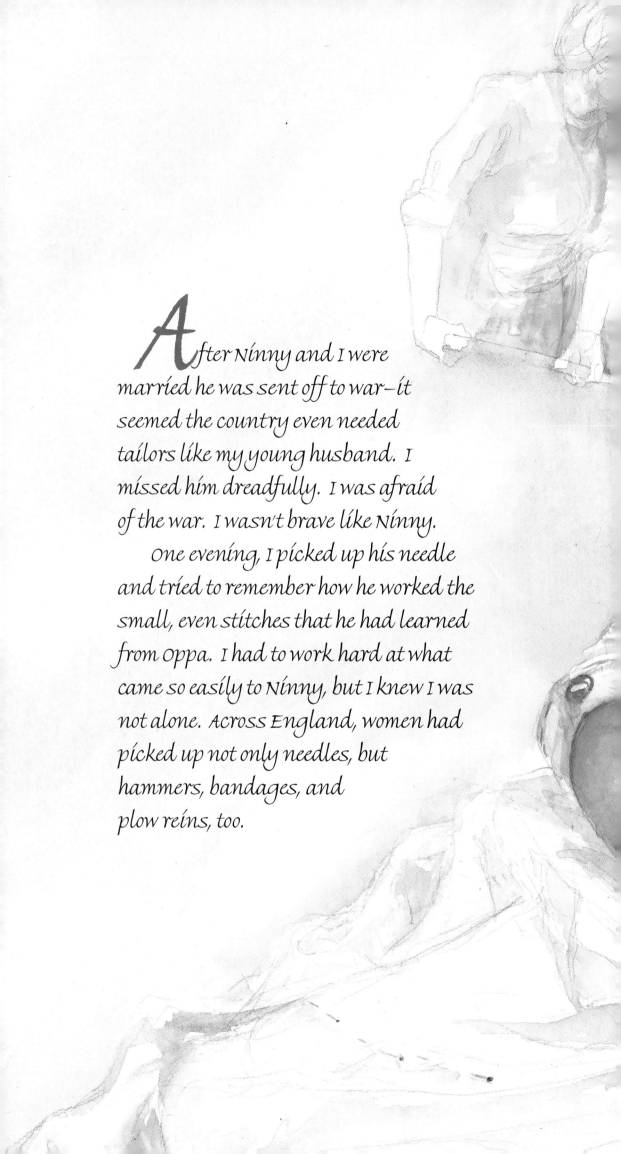

After Ninny and I were married he was sent off to war—it seemed the country even needed tailors like my young husband. I missed him dreadfully. I was afraid of the war. I wasn't brave like Ninny.

One evening, I picked up his needle and tried to remember how he worked the small, even stitches that he had learned from Oppa. I had to work hard at what came so easily to Ninny, but I knew I was not alone. Across England, women had picked up not only needles, but hammers, bandages, and plow reins, too.

D-Day was a surprise. The Normandy invasion was a secret.

As news broke out of the Allied landing, I grew worried. It had been weeks since a letter had arrived from Ninny. Each night I sat on the worn wooden steps that led to the garden.

Waiting.

From there I watched our son, Edward, rollop in the moonlight. Beyond him, past the fields of barley and rye, lay the graveyard.

I sang softly as I watched the stars
watching Ninny—

Ninny! Oh, Ninny!
Come dance with me!
    For I'd hate to dance alone,
    Where the old men sleep,
        And the women weep,
        And the wild, fey
            children roam.

Many men died at Normandy. No one knew the fate of their husbands, fathers, or sons. For days, the wind was filled with the voices of a thousand women.

Women who feared the graveyard, just like me.

Each day I listened for the sound of buttons
against my windowpane, telling me that
Ninny was alive–and home safely.
Instead it was old McKinney's bicycle wheels
crunching the gravel that brought me word
of Ninny.

*B*essie! Oh, Bessie!
Come dance with me!
        For I hate to dance alone,
where the old men sleep,
        And the women weep,
And the wild, fey
                children roam.

Ninny was dancing with a dishrag as
I cleared sticky teacakes from their trays.
    "No time for dancing tonight, Ninny-boy!
This party is for US." It was our anniversary
and all of the children had come to celebrate.
    "Then who else but us should be dancing?"
laughed Ninny. "Look, Bessie. It's just like
our song—"
    We peeked into the parlor and there was
old Uncle Wendell, snoring in Ninny's favorite
armchair, amid a roving band of grandchildren.
And Edward's wife, Dede, was crying into her
kerchief saying "It's beautiful, Edward. Isn't
it beautiful?"
    It WAS just like our song.

"Dance with me, Bessie,"
whispered Ninny.
    I nodded and closed my eyes.
    Then his arm circled my waist
and we slipped out into the
garden. My dear old Ninny
suddenly seemed almost spry.
    It was an enchanted night
like thousands I'd spent with
Ninny. Not once did our feet
stumble. We never missed a step.

"Open your eyes, Bessie."

Ninny had stopped dancing and was looking toward the graveyard. There stood Oppa's gravestone, bathed in moonlight. He was still watching over us. I looked at Ninny with wonder.

HE TAUGHT US
TO SING
TO DANCE
TO TELL STORIES

"I think
Oppa would
have had
a grand time
tonight, Ninny,"
I said softly.

"What makes you think he
isn't?" he grinned. Our feet moved
like old friends as we began to
dance again. Ninny leaned close
and said, "When it's time, Bessie,
remember our promise to each
other, and save the last
dance for me."

I am an old woman now.

On nights when the moon sits full-bellied
on the treetops, I am reminded that I have a
promise to keep.
I no longer fear the graveyard. Any place
my Ninny sleeps is a good place.